THE
NUTMEG PRINCESS

THE
NUTMEG PRINCESS

written by
Richardo Keens-Douglas
illustrated by
Annouchka Galouchko

annick press
Toronto • New York • Vancouver

Annick Press Ltd.

We acknowledge the support of the Canada Council for the Arts, the Ontario Arts Council, and the Government of Canada through the Canada Book Fund (CBF) for our publishing activities.

Cataloging in Publication
Keens-Douglas, Richardo, author
        The nutmeg princess / written by Richardo
Keens-Douglas ; illustrated by Annouchka Galouchko.
— New edition.

ISBN 978-1-55451-600-1 (bound).—ISBN 978-1-55451-599-8 (pbk.)

        I. Gravel Galouchko, Annouchka, 1960-, illustrator
II. Title.

PS8571.E44545N88 2014   jC813'.54   C2013-903578-8

Distributed in Canada by:
Firefly Books Ltd.
50 Staples Avenue, Unit 1
Richmond Hill, ON L4B 0A7

Published in the U.S.A. by Annick Press (U.S.) Ltd.
Distributed in the U.S.A. by:
Firefly Books (U.S.) Inc.
P.O. Box 1338
Ellicott Station
Buffalo, NY 14205

Printed in China
Visit us at: www.annickpress.com
Visit Annouchka Galouchko at: www.annouchka.ca

In loving memory of my mother,
the original Nutmeg Princess

On a little island in the Caribbean called the Isle of Spice, there lived an old lady way up in the mountains. Petite Mama was tiny, but she worked hard and was very strong. She owned lots of land where she grew bananas, soursops, oranges, star-apples, mangoes, and every other tropical fruit you could think of. When they were ripe, she would go down the mountain to sell her fruits in the town. No one would come up the mountain to buy from Petite Mama because people were afraid of her. They thought she was some kind of witch.

P etite Mama had many fruit trees, but her choicest crop came from the nutmeg. Just beyond her nutmeg trees was a bottomless lake in the middle of a volcano. Now, on this lake, Petite Mama said, lived a beautiful young woman. Petite Mama called her the Nutmeg Princess because she would only appear when the nutmeg was ready for picking.

Dressed in a pale blue gown, with dew drops in her hair that looked like diamonds, she would sit on a bamboo raft in the middle of the lake humming a song, sometimes sad, sometimes happy, and in the blink of an eye, she would disappear.

Petite Mama was the only one who had ever seen her.

In the town lived a boy named Aglo and his best friend, a girl named Petal. Aglo and Petal loved to spend time with each other. Sometimes they would splash in the ocean. Other times they played hide-and-seek among the colorful trees and bushes. But what they loved most was reading together.

Whenever they saw Petite Mama selling her fruits, they would call out, "Do you want any help today, Petite Mama?" And she would shout back, "No thanks, children, not today."

Some days Petite Mama would surprise them and throw them a couple of mangoes or plums. They would bite into the fruit and laugh as the sweet juices trickled down their chins.

One day, Aglo went all the way up the mountain to see Petite Mama.

"Is there really a Nutmeg Princess?" he asked. "I would like to see her. The nutmeg is beginning to bloom and she should appear soon."

"Do you believe I see her?" Petite Mama asked.

"Oh yes, Petite Mama, I believe you."

"Then get up bright and early in the morning. When you hear the first cock crow, start to climb the mountain until you reach the lake. Sit down on the big stone by the old red row-boat and wait."

"Will she come?" asked Aglo.

"Only the good Lord knows, my child."

With that, Aglo ran down the mountain straight to Petal's house. Petal agreed to go with him.

V ery early the next morning, Aglo and Petal were halfway up the mountain when they heard the first cock crow. Up and up they went until at last they came to the small lake. The smell of nutmeg was very strong, drifting back and forth in the fresh morning breeze.

Suddenly everything became very still.

"Look," Aglo said quietly, pointing to the raft. "There she is."

"Where, where?" Petal shouted.

But no matter where Petal looked, she couldn't see the princess.

W hat is she like, Aglo?"
asked Petal.

"She's very beautiful.
She's wearing a long blue dress. She
has diamonds in her hair, and she's
smiling at us. Oh! She's gone, Petal.
She's gone."

"I wish I could have seen her," said
Petal, disappointed.

"Maybe next time," replied Aglo.

They ran back down the mountain,
stopping at Petite Mama's house to
tell her the good news. Down they
continued, shouting that they had
seen the Nutmeg Princess, but no one
believed Aglo, except Petal and Petite
Mama.

Although nobody else believed Aglo, half the town still came up the mountain to sit by the lake. If what Aglo said was true and the princess had all those diamonds in her hair, the townspeople thought they would get some and be rich for the rest of their lives.

After two days, the princess had not appeared.

Then on the third morning, everything became very still.

here she is!" exclaimed Aglo.

"Where? Where?" shouted everyone.

All they could see was the bamboo raft.

"Maybe the diamonds are on the raft," said a lady. And with that, they all jumped into the water and swam toward the raft.

The Nutmeg Princess stood there singing her sad song. She saw how the people only cared for riches and nothing else. And then she signalled Aglo and Petal to come to her.

"But I can't swim!" cried Aglo.

"Let's use this old rowboat," said Petal.

Off they went, rowing toward the princess. But halfway there, the boat started to leak and slowly began to sink.

"I can't swim!" Aglo called out in a panic.

"Don't worry," replied Petal. "Just hold on to me and everything will be all right."

Petal swam with Aglo holding on to her until, all wet and exhausted, they reached the raft.

"Is she here?" Petal asked as they climbed up.

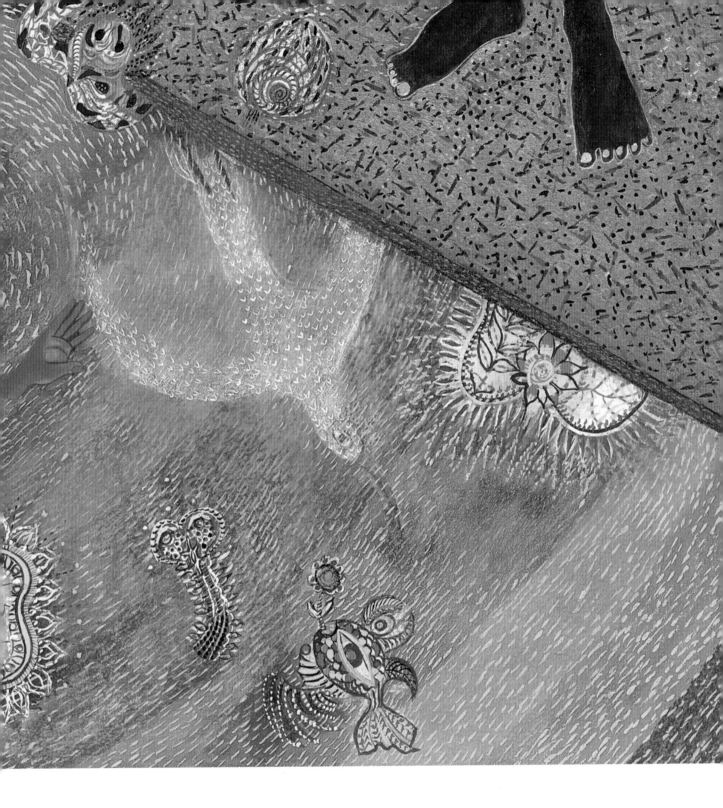

"She is and she is smiling at us," said Aglo.

As for the townspeople, whenever they got close, the raft would drift out of reach until they all got tired and swam back to shore.

Suddenly, the princess shook her hair, scattering her dew drop diamonds all over the lake. It was as if the heavens had opened and were raining millions of stars. One diamond landed in the middle of Petal's forehead.

"I can see her, Aglo. I can see her!" shouted Petal.

The Princess looked at Petal. "You cared enough for your friend to bring him to safety. Take that gift of caring out into the world, and remember, if you believe in yourself all things are possible." And she was gone.

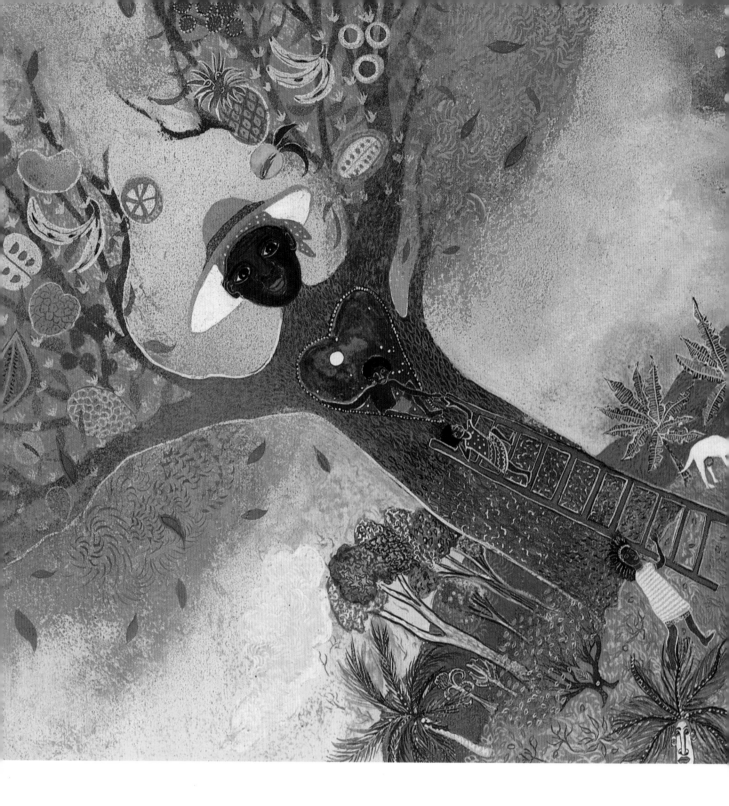

Aglo and Petal went back down the mountain, straight to Petite Mama's house. But Petite Mama was gone, too.

She had left a letter, and this is what it said:

"I leave my entire estate to Petal and Aglo. I know they will keep my fruit and my nutmeg trees growing for generations to come."

Today, because of Petal and Aglo's hard work, the nutmeg is the most precious crop on that little island in the Caribbean, the Isle of Spice.

As for the Nutmeg Princess and Petite Mama, no one has ever seen them again.

Richardo Keens-Douglas, actor, broadcaster, and writer of plays, songs, and children's stories, is, above all, a storyteller. Born in Grenada where he spent much of his childhood, Keens-Douglas was largely inspired by the oral storytelling tradition on the island. What he enjoys most is sharing his stories during workshops in schools and universities, and encouraging the use of imagination and the expression of cultural pride.

Keens-Douglas's first book for children, *The Nutmeg Princess*, was published by Annick Press in 1992. It came about as a result of a school visit where a little girl put up her hand and asked if he knew a story about a black princess. At the time, he didn't, but it was all he needed to inspire him to write *The Nutmeg Princess*, which was followed by many other books with multicultural themes. His musical adaptation of *The Nutmeg Princess* won the 1999 Dora Mavor Moore award for outstanding new musical.

Keens-Douglas currently divides his time between Toronto and Grenada.

Annouchka Gravel Galouchko was born in Montreal. As a child, she lived in many foreign countries including Iran, Egypt, Mexico, and Austria.

From her earliest childhood, Galouchko loved to paint and sculpt. By her early twenties, she had developed her unique style of painting and held several exhibitions. She gained formal training at the University of Quebec, obtaining her Bachelor of Fine Arts in 1990.

The Nutmeg Princess was her first published book. From the start, Galouchko felt a spiritual connection with the story: "I turned to photographs and the library for information on the Caribbean. My traveling experiences helped a lot." Her pictures are colorful, multi-sensory, mystical, and complex, reflecting layers of understanding.

Galouchko lives in Montreal with her partner, artist Stéphan Daigle, who often collaborates with her on her art.